The Little Mermaid

MILES KELLY

Deep beneath the ocean, where
the water is emerald blue,
lived the Sea King
– a merman – and
all his subjects.

He lived with his daughters, the little sea princesses, in a beautiful castle made of coral, shells and pearls.

The youngest mermaid was much quieter than her sisters and longed for the world above the waves.

She could often be fou[n]
gazing at a statue of [a]
man that had fallen t[o the]
sea floor from a w[reck]

One evening, a large ship with three masts lay on
the water. There was music and song on board
and as night fell, coloured lanterns were lit.

The little mermaid
swam closer to get a
better look at the people
onboard. Inside was a young
prince. He was having a

birthday party!

Everyone was dancing, having fun.
Then there were fireworks, which
exploded as bright as day.

But all of a sudden a storm was upon them! The ship groaned and creaked as the waves broke over the deck.

Everyone was in grave danger!

The little mermaid saw
the prince slip into the water.
Rising and falling with the
waves, she reached him, and
dragged him to the surface.

The little mermaid swam through the night to find land, and eventually she found a little bay, near a castle, where the water was deep.

She pushed the prince onto the warm, dry sand.

Suddenly a princess appeared from the castle. She hurried towards the prince.

The little mermaid hid behind some rocks, and watched from the water.

The princess helped
the prince back to
her father's castle
to recover.

They soon
fell in love.

Even so, the prince
couldn't help but wonder
who had saved him.

Each day the mermaid returned
to the bay. She would hide
and watch as the prince rowed
his rowing boat every evening.

One day, a great party was held at the Sea King's palace. Everyone was dancing and singing – all apart from the little mermaid.

She was desperate to find a
way to be with her prince,
so she left to find the
old sea witch.

The old sea witch
smiled nastily when
the little mermaid
asked to be given
legs to replace her

**mermaid's
tail.**

"If you drink this potion your wish will be granted – but if the prince marries another, you must return to the sea and become foam on the waves."

"As payment, you will lose your voice!" she added.

The little mermaid swam to the shore and drank the potion. At once, her tail became two legs. She tried to find the prince but found it hard to walk.

The little mermaid sat down to rest and soon fell fast asleep. When she awoke, the prince was there. "I'll take care of you," he said.

But the little mermaid couldn't reply.

They spent lots of time together and
the little mermaid fell even more in
love. But the prince was engaged to be
married to the princess who had
found him on the shore.

On the day of the prince's wedding the little mermaid was very sad indeed. She left the ceremony to return to the sea, but she did not turn to foam, as the sea witch had said.

Instead, she found herself being lifted up by spirits. "Don't be sad. Come with us!" they cried. "We fly around the world to do good deeds!" The little mermaid joined them and was happy at last.